SAFARI FIELD GUIDE

Activities, Doodling, and Fun Facts

Written by Cynthia Stierle

Silver Dolphin

San Diego, California

Finish the Photo

It's great to take pictures while you're on safari, but parts of this photo are missing. Finish the photo by matching each piece shown below to the correct spot in the scene. Write the corresponding number next to each piece. (Answer on page 2

rack the Trail

A lion cub stays with its mother until it's at least two years old. But this lion cub has wandered off and is lost. Which of the three trails will lead it back to its mother? (Answer on page 22.)

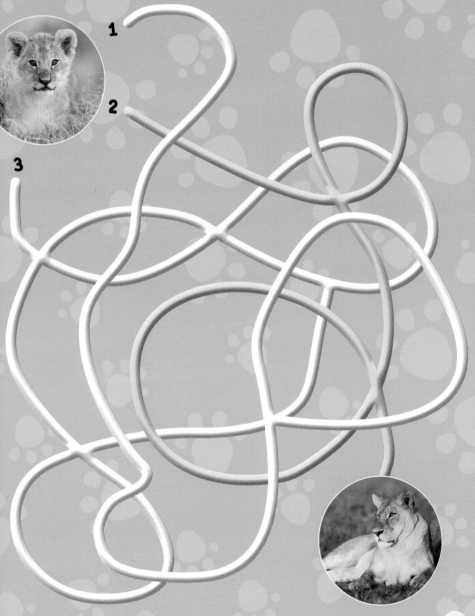

What's Different?

The lake is a great stop on the safari, because many different animals gather there during the dry season. Look at the two pictures. There are five differences between them. Can you fin them all? (Answers on page 22.)

What do you see that is different?

1. _____

2. _____

3. _____

4. _____

5. _____

Shadow Cats

Look at the shadows at the bottom of the page and match them to the big cats at the top. (Answers on page 22.)

1. Leopard

2. Caracal cat

3. Lion

4. Cheetah

A.

B.

C.

D.

Lost on Safari

Four animals are missing from the grid below. Each animal should appear once in each column and once in each row. Use the stickers that came with this book to fill in the grid with the "lost" animals. (Answer on page 22.)

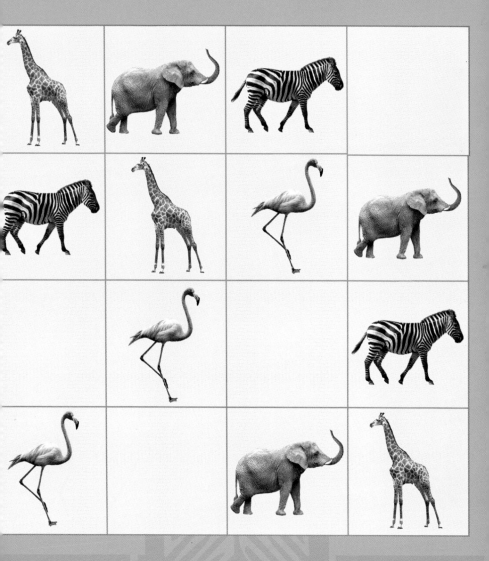

Scene on the Savanna

The savanna grasslands are home for many different animals. But where are they? Use the stickers that came with this book to add animals and make an incredible safari scene.

Identifying Animals

Most of the animals you see on a safari are very well known. Can you recognize them all? Look at the pictures and fill in the boxes with the names of the animals in the pictures. We've done the first one for you. (Answer on page 22.)

| F | L | A | M | I | N | G | O |

elephant   ostrich   rhinoceros
zebra   flamingo   lion
giraffe   cheetah   baboon

ACROSS

1

3

6

8

9

DOWN

2

4

5

7

What Do You See?

What animal would you most like to see on your safari?
Draw a picture of it.

Paw Print Code

See if you can read the animal tracks. Look at the paw prints at the top of the page. Each print represents a letter. Use this key to fill in the blanks on the lines below to reveal the answer to the question. (Answer on page 22.)

F   T   D   O   S   A

Question: What did the cheetah have for dinner?

_____   _____   _____   _____

_____   _____   _____   _____

Same Stripes

Though zebras might look the same, the pattern of stripes on each one is different. But one zebra on the left is exactly the same as a zebra on the right. Look at the pictures on both pages. Can you find the matching pair? (Answer on page 22.)

River Maze

Wildebeest have to cross rivers when they migrate, but they need to watch out for crocodiles. Help the wildebeest find a way to get safely across the river. (Answer on page 22.)

Wish You Were Here!

Send some pictures and postcards to tell people about your adventures. Draw pictures of your favorite animals in the phot frames. Then write a few words to explain why those animals are your favorites—and why everyone should go on safari!

Why everyone should go on safari:

_____

_____

_____

_____

Answers

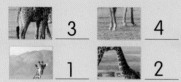

3 4

1 2

PAGE 5:

1
2
3

PAGES 6-7:

PAGE 8:

1. B   2. D   3. C   4. A

PAGE 9:

PAGES 12-13:

¹F L A M I N ²G O
              I R
          ³Z E ⁴B R A F F
              A   F
              B   F
          ⁵C O
          ⁶R H I N O C E R ⁷O S
          E   N   S
          E   T
          T   R
          A   ⁸L I O N
          H   C
                    ⁹E L E P H A N T

PAGE 15:

F   A   S   T

F   O   O   D

PAGES 16-17

PAGES 18-19

22